I read this book all by myself

....

For Toby – JW
For Luke – GP

A Red Fox Book

Published by Random House Children's Books
61-63 Uxbridge Road, London W5 5SA
A division of the Random House Group Ltd

Addresses for companies within The Random House Group Limited
can be found at : www.randomhouse.co.uk/offices.htm

5 7 9 10 8 6

First published in Great Britain by Red Fox 2001

Published in hardback by Heinemann Library, a division of
Reed Educational and Professional Publishing Limited,
by arrangement with Random House Children's Books

Printed in Singapore by Tien Wah Press

THE RANDOM HOUSE GROUP Limited Reg. No. 954009
www.kidsatrandomhouse.co.uk

ISBN 978 0 09 941742 2

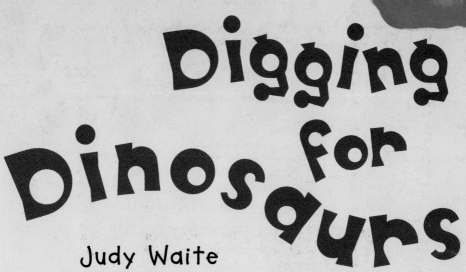

Digging for Dinosaurs

Judy Waite

Garry Parsons

RED FOX

Dan was reading his favourite book.
"I want to dig for dinosaurs,"
he said suddenly.

Dan's dog, Bouncer, bounced over to him.
Dan ruffled Bouncer's ears.

"Let's start with the garden," he said.

"Don't get muddy," warned Mum. "I've planned a trip to the museum."

Dan didn't answer. He knew he'd hate the museum. Museums were musty, smelly and dusty.

Soon Dan was digging a deep, dark hole.
"I'm going two hundred and twenty-five
million years deep," he told Bouncer.

He felt a bubble of excitement. Wouldn't
it be brilliant to really find a dinosaur?
He wondered if he'd recognise it if he did.

Bouncer scratched
at the edge of the
hole. A sprinkle of
mud slid back into it.

"Don't do that," groaned Dan. "I've just dug down to the Cretaceous period. I might be about to find the remains of a terrible Tyrannosaurus rex that could swallow a boy in just two bites."

The hole grew
deeper and darker.

Dan found a
stone – like an
odd sort of bone.

But he didn't find the remains of a terrible Tyrannosaurus rex that could swallow a boy in just two bites.

Mum called to Dan, "We're going in ten minutes!"

We're going in ten minutes!

Dan growled
his grumpiest
Tyrannosaurus growl.

He threw the odd
looking stone for
Bouncer to chase.
Museums were
boring. Like old
people snoring.

Bouncer came bouncing
back. He dropped the
stone into the hole.
A slither of mud
trickled down
on top of it.

"Don't do that," groaned Dan. "I've just dug down to the Jurassic period. I might be about to find the remains of a gigantic Brachiosaurus that was taller than the tallest trees."

Dan kept on digging. The hole grew deeper and darker.

Dan found a peg, and a pin,

and a scrunched-up old tin.

18

But he didn't find the remains of a gigantic Brachiosaurus that was taller than the tallest trees.

"I hope you're not getting too mucky," called Mum. "We're off in five minutes."

Dan stamped his foot like a bad-tempered Brachiosaurus. He threw the odd looking stone for Bouncer to chase.

Museums were sleepy, crummy and creepy.

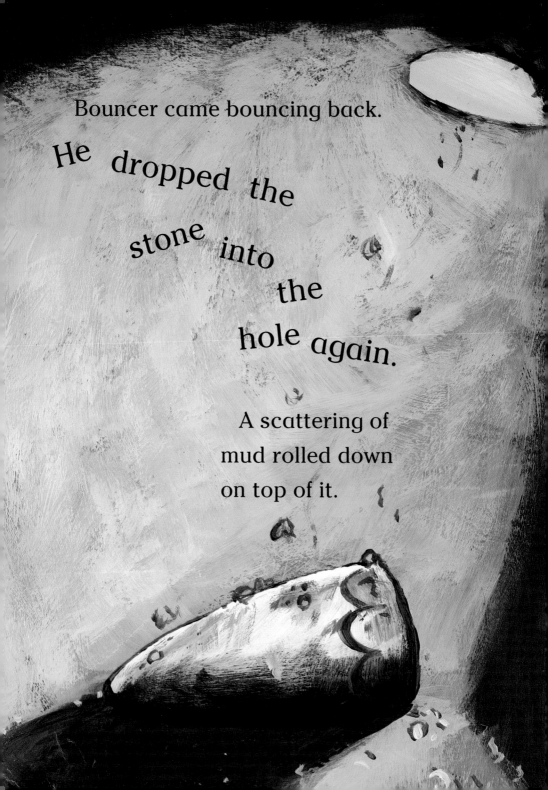

Bouncer came bouncing back.

He dropped the
stone into
the
hole again.

A scattering of
mud rolled down
on top of it.

"Don't do that," groaned Dan. "I've just dug all the way down to the Triassic period. I might be about to find the remains of the crazy Coelophysis that had knife-sharp teeth and sometimes ate its own young."

Dan kept on
digging. The hole
grew deeper and darker.

Dan found an old plate and the key to a gate. But he didn't find the remains of the crazy Coelophysis that had knife-sharp teeth and sometimes ate its own young.

Mum appeared suddenly. "You're covered in mud," she said crossly. "Go inside and get cleaned up. It's time to go."

Dan made his craziest Coelophysis face.
He threw the odd looking stone
for Bouncer to chase.
Museums were old,
crusty and cold.

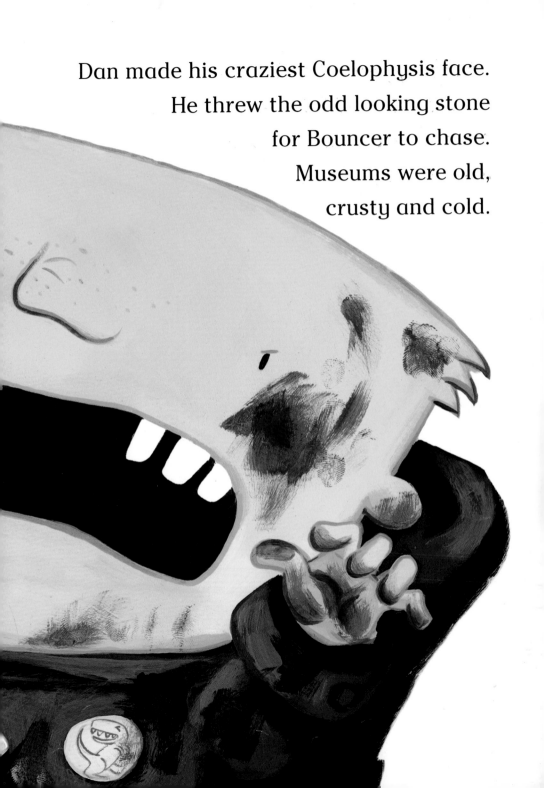

Bouncer came
bouncing back.
He dropped the
stone into the
hole again. A
shower of mud
pattered down on
top of it.

"Come on, Dan,"
said Mum.
Dan growled
and stamped
and gnashed his
dinosaur teeth.

Then he turned to Bouncer,
"Go on then, bury your bone
in my hole. Digging for
dinosaurs was a stupid
idea anyway."

He stomped away into the house.

In the bathroom, Dan stared into the mirror. He had a front tooth missing, and he stuck his tongue through the gap.

He thought about how some dinosaurs grew new teeth when the old ones got broken.

Then he practised his angry dinosaur
face in the mirror.

Mum peered round the
door, "Hurry up!"
she grumbled.

Mum drove to the museum. Dan looked out of the back window and imagined a world full of dinosaurs.

He pictured them wandering wild amongst vast mountains and plains.

He heard snorts. He heard roars.

He saw great
grabbing claws . . .

"We're here," said Mum, pulling into
the museum car park.
   Dan trailed behind Mum
into the museum.

And when he got inside – he was surprised.

No one was bored, nobody snored. No one was sleepy, nothing seemed creepy.

It wasn't cold, and it wasn't old.
It was all fresh and new,
with zillions to do.

It had fossils
and stones . . .

. . . and some brilliant bones.

Dan stared and stared
at the Tyrannosaurus rex.
Monster sized questions
rose up in his mind.

How fast could it run?

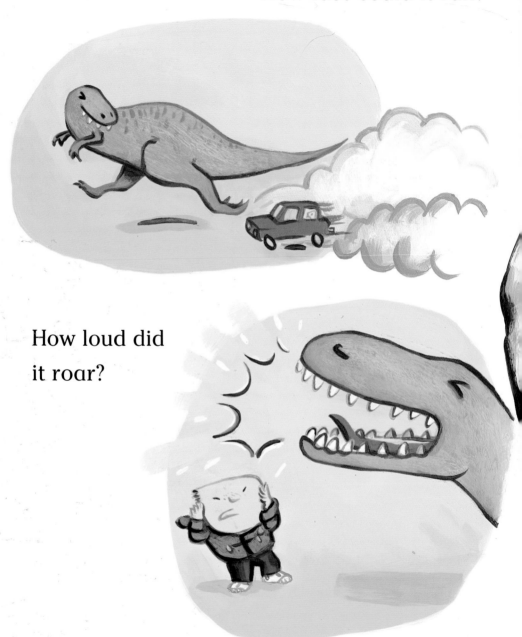

How loud did
it roar?

What would it be like to see those giant jaws really begin to open . . .

"Just look at those fearsome fangs," said Mum.

"There's one missing!" cried Dan. "It's got a gap in its mouth – just like me."

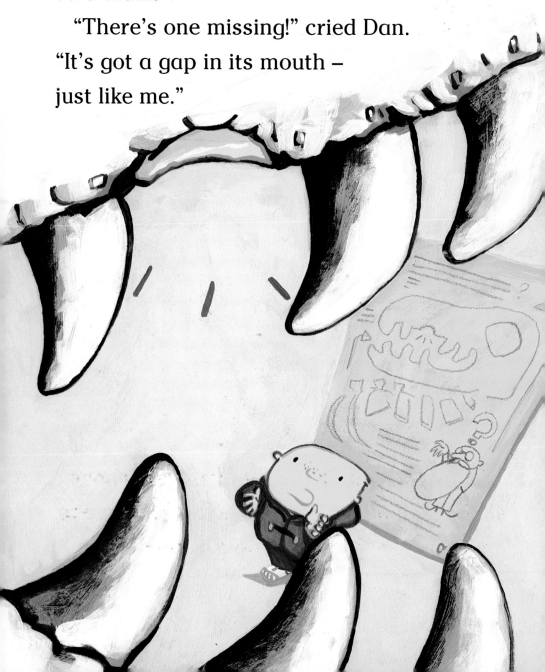

Dan could see the sort of shape the missing tooth would be. He could see the sort of size the missing tooth would be.

He gave Mum his most gigantic dinosaur smile, "I've had a great time, but we have to go home. I've got to dig up an odd looking stone . . ."

Can you help Dan make a T-rex skeleton like the one in the museum? What others can you make?

You will need: nine pipe cleaners

1. HEAD, BODY, AND TAIL: twist the ends of two pipe cleaners together and shape into a curve.

2. TOP OF HEAD: curve the end of the first pipe cleaner round. Shape into zigzag teeth.

4. FRONT LEGS: fold a pipe cleaner in half and join its middle onto the body, just below the head. Fold the ends in half again.

3. LOWER JAW: zigzag the end of a pipe cleaner into teeth and loop it under. Twist the long end onto the body.

5. RIBS: twist three pipe cleaners into circles. Cross the ends over and twist them onto the body.

6. BACK LEGS: twist two pipe cleaners onto either side of the body. Shape the ends into flat feet with three toes so that your dinosaur stands up.

*Hint: make sure you wind the pipe cleaners tightly around each other!

Massive head with large jaws to crush prey

I eat plant-eating dinosaurs. Yum, yum!

Tiny arms

Powerful legs

T-rex Tooth
(As long as a grown-up's hand)

Pointed teeth with sharp edges like saws were good for eating meat. Dinosaur teeth grew back when they wore down.

Tyrannosaurus rex (tie-ranna-saw-rus rex) was one of the largest meat eaters. It was a carnosaur, or "flesh lizard". It was so heavy it couldn't run fast for very long. So it waited for its prey and attacked quickly.

45

Meet the author.

Judy Waite

How did you get the idea for this story? When my two daughters were young, they loved digging for treasure. They found all sorts of things – odd shaped stones, buttons, tins . . . They would bring their treasure home and play 'museums'. We also had a dog called Clarrie, who loved chasing sticks and burying them. These memories gave me the idea for this story. Then I went to the library and found out all about dinosaurs.

Did you write when you were little? I have always loved writing. I grew up in a country called Singapore, and because it was so hot, we only had to go to school in the mornings. I think having all that time to play helped my imagination to grow, so I thought up lots of stories.

Can I be a writer like you? Don't wait until your teacher asks for a story – write for your mum, your little brother, or even your goldfish. Make comics. Read a lot. Enter story writing competitions. The more you write, the better you will be.

Garry Parsons

Meet the illustrator.

How did you do the pictures in this book? The pictures are painted in acrylic paints, with some coloured pencil scribbles. I painted all the pictures at the same time and they took four weeks non-stop to finish.

Did you know all about dinosaurs? Yes, I loved dinosaurs when I was young, especially Tyrannosaurus rex and Diplodocus. I liked comparing their sizes to buses and people and imagining them in the garden.

Have you ever seen a dinosaur skeleton? Yes, in the Natural History Museum in London. It's like the museum Dan visits and has lots of dinosaurs you can see close-up.

What did you like to do when you were a child? I liked to imagine volcanoes erupting in the garden, and to make things from scraps of paper.

How can I be an illustrator like you? Take a notebook everywhere and draw. Imagine dinosaurs in your street – draw them!

Will you try and write or draw a story?

47

Let your ideas take flight with
Flying Foxes

All the Little Ones – and a Half
by Mary Murphy

Sherman Swaps Shells
by Jane Clarke and Ant Parker

Digging for Dinosaurs
by Judy Waite and Garry Parsons

Shadowhog
by Sandra Ann Horn and Mary McQuillan

The Magic Backpack
by Julia Jarman and Adriano Gon

Jake and the Red Bird
by Ragnhild Scamell and Valeria Petrone